Old Mother Hubbard's Stolen Bone

First published in 2009
by Wayland

Text copyright © Alan Durant 2009
Illustration copyright © Leah-Ellen Heming 2009

Wayland
338 Euston Road
London NW1 3BH

Wayland Australia
Level 17/207 Kent Street
Sydney, NSW 2000

Series Editor: Louise John
Editor: Katie Powell
Cover design: Paul Cherrill
Design: D.R.ink
Consultant: Shirley Bickler

A CIP catalogue record for this book is available from the British Library.

ISBN 9780750256018

Printed in China

Wayland is a division of Hachette Children's Books,
an Hachette Livre UK company

www.hachettelivre.co.uk

Old Mother Hubbard's Stolen Bone

Written by Alan Durant
Illustrated by Leah-Ellen Heming

WAYLAND

Old Mother Hubbard had a dog, a very clever dog. He did tricks. He could lie down with his paws in the air and play dead.

He could dance and stand on his front paws. He could open doors and shut them again.

"What a clever boy!" said Old Mother Hubbard. How she loved that dog!

One morning she went to the butcher's and bought her dog a big juicy bone for a treat. She put the bone in the cupboard.

Then she went out in the garden to peg out the washing.

When she came back, her dog
was doing cartwheels. Old Mother
Hubbard laughed.

"What a clever boy!" she said, and she
went to the cupboard to fetch her dog
the bone.

But when she opened the door,
the cupboard was bare!
"I've been robbed!" she cried. Her
poor dog covered his eyes with his
paws and howled.

"Don't you worry, boy," said Old
Mother Hubbard. "I'll catch that
bone thief!"

Old Mother Hubbard ran out into the street and oof! She bumped into Simple Simon. He was carrying something in a leather bag.

"Did you steal my bone?" Old Mother Hubbard demanded.

"Indeed, no!" said Simple Simon. "I've got lots of bones of my own. See." He pointed to his head, his arms and his legs.

"Not those sort of bones, you dolt,"
said Old Mother Hubbard. "I mean
the bone I bought for my dog to eat."
She glared at Simple Simon. "Show me
what's in your bag."

12

Simple Simon opened his bag and took out a chicken pie. "I bought it from a pieman going to the fair," he said. "It cost me one penny."

"Bah!" huffed Old Mother Hubbard and on she ran.

At the corner of the street was Little Jack Horner, sitting on the pavement, eating.

When he saw Old Mother Hubbard, he hid the food behind his back.

"Did you steal my dog's bone?" cried
Old Mother Hubbard.
"N-n-no," stammered Little Jack. "Not I."
"Show me what's behind your back,"
she commanded.

Little Jack Horner put his hands behind
him and brought out a Christmas pie.

Then he put in his thumb, and pulled out a plum, and said, "What a clever boy am I!"

"Bah!" huffed Old Mother Hubbard
and on she ran.

Old Mother Hubbard came to Jack Sprat's house. He and his wife were sitting at the table, munching.

Old Mother Hubbard put her head through the window.

"Are you eating my dog's bone?"
she demanded.
"Certainly not!" humphed Jack Sprat.
"I'm eating the lean of the meat."

"And I'm eating the fat," said his wife.
"But neither of us would ever eat bones!"
"Bah!" huffed Old Mother Hubbard.

Suddenly there was a commotion
behind her.

"Stop, thief!" someone shouted.

Old Mother Hubbard turned to see the Knave of Hearts sprinting past her, carrying a basket with the queen chasing after him.

"Stop, thief!" the queen shouted again.

"I bet that naughty knave stole my
dog's bone," said Old Mother Hubbard
to herself, and off she ran after the
knave and the queen.

Old Mother Hubbard and the queen chased the knave through the town, upstairs and downstairs and into the lady's chamber...

over Margery Daw's see-saw...

and past lavender blue and lavender green...

until, finally, they caught him in the wood where red herrings grow. "Give me back my bone!" cried Old Mother Hubbard.

"But I didn't steal your bone," said the Knave of Hearts.

"No, you stole my tarts," said
the queen.

"Sorry," said the knave. "They were so
delicious — and I was very hungry."

The queen forgave the knave. "As we're in the wood, we may as well have a picnic," she said, and she passed round the tarts.

"A very good idea," agreed Old Mother Hubbard.

So, Old Mother Hubbard, the queen and the Knave of Hearts sat and ate until all the tarts were gone.

"It's still a mystery who stole that bone," said Old Mother Hubbard. But she was so full of delicious jam tarts that she wasn't really that bothered any more.

She said farewell and walked back
home...

...and there was her dog, chewing his way through that stolen bone. What a naughty dog!

START READING is a series of highly enjoyable books for beginner readers. **The books have been carefully graded to match the Book Bands widely used in schools.** This enables readers to be sure they choose books that match their own reading ability.

Look out for the Band colour on the book in our Start Reading logo.

The Bands are:

Pink Band 1
Red Band 2
Yellow Band 3
Blue Band 4
Green Band 5
Orange Band 6
Turquoise Band 7
Purple Band 8
Gold Band 9

START READING books can be read independently or shared with an adult. They promote the enjoyment of reading through satisfying stories supported by fun illustrations.

Alan Durant has written many stories and poems for children of all ages. He loves nursery rhymes and often makes up his own like this one:
I met a funny author / He was scribbling in his book.
I asked, "What are you writing?" / But he wouldn't let me look.

Leah-Ellen Heming once brought back a mouse from her studio in her backpack and cycled it all the way up a very steep hill to her house, where it escaped. The mouse then had a big family, but Leah caught them all and unleashed the mice in her friend's allotment, where they now live happily ever after.